T0163047

TOGETHER FOREVER

The story about the magician
who didn't want to be alone

LAITMAN
KABBALAH PUBLISHERS

Michael Laitman

TOGETHER FOREVER

The story about the magician
who didn't want to be alone

Illustrations: Tzezar Orshanski
Layout: Rami Yaniv
Translation: Chaim Ratz
Associate Editors: Debbie Sirt, Tony Kosinec, Susan Morales Kosinec
Copy Editor: Claire Gerus
Printing: Doron Goldin

Post Production: Uri Laitman

Executive Editor: Chaim Ratz

ISBN 978-1-897448-12-0

FIRST EDITION: NOVEMBER 2008

First printing

Do you know why old folks are the best tellers of legends?
It's because a legend is the cleverest thing on earth!
Everything in the world changes, but true legends always stay.

Legends are filled with so much wisdom, that to tell them,
a person needs to see things that others miss.
It takes a long, long time to gain
so much wisdom,
and that's why older folks often
tell legends better than anyone else!

As it is written in the greatest,
most ancient magical book,
The Book of Zohar,
"An old person is one
who has acquired wisdom."

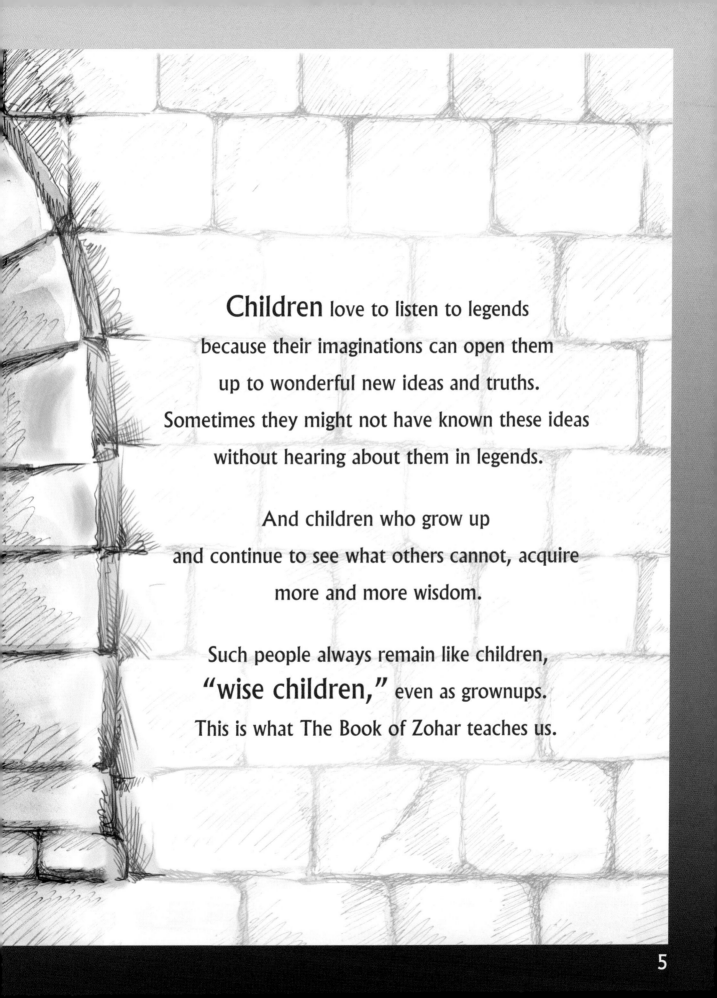

Children love to listen to legends
because their imaginations can open them
up to wonderful new ideas and truths.
Sometimes they might not have known these ideas
without hearing about them in legends.

And children who grow up
and continue to see what others cannot, acquire
more and more wisdom.

Such people always remain like children,
"wise children," even as grownups.
This is what The Book of Zohar teaches us.

There once was
a great magician,
kind, generous,
and goodhearted.

But unlike all other good
magicians in children's legends,
this magician was so very kind,
he missed having
someone to share
his goodness with...

He had no one to love or care for,
and no one to play with,
to be with,
or to think about.

Besides,
he longed for someone
to know him and to care about him...

...because it's very sad to be alone.
So what did he do?

He thought to himself:
"I know! I'll make a pebble,
a tiny one, but very beautiful.
I will gently hold it and stroke it,
and feel it always by my side.
And we will be together,
the pebble and I, because...

it's very sad to be alone."

He waved his magic stick, and CHACK!

a pretty little pebble rested in the good magician's hand.

He stroked the smooth little pebble and wrapped it lovingly in his warm palm. He spoke lovingly to it, but the stone didn't answer. It just lay there in his hand, motionless and silent.

And worst of all, it did not return his love.

No matter what he did to it,
the stone would not become friendly,
or even react at all.

He thought, "Is this the way to treat a good magician?
How come the sweet-looking pebble isn't responding?
Maybe there is something wrong with it?
Perhaps I should make more pebbles,
and maybe they will be friendlier
and return my friendship?"

So the magician made
more pebbles, then larger stones:
rocks, hills, mountains, the Earth,
and even the whole universe.

But they were all like the first pebble:
they didn't move,
didn't speak, and just
didn't respond at all.

And once again he felt
how sad it was to be alone.

In his sadness he wondered,

"Perhaps I should make a plant instead?
Yes, a very beautiful flower!

I'll water it, give it lots of fresh air,
beam down warm sunshine,
and play sweet music to it.

The plant will be so happy,
and then we'll both be happy because…

it's very sad to be alone."

The good magician waved his magic stick again, and CHACK!

a pretty little flower appeared right next to his chair. With its rosy petals and long and gentle leaves, the flower looked exactly as he pictured it.

The magician was so excited he began to skip and hop around it, and sang the most cheerful songs he knew. But the plant wouldn't dance with him; it wouldn't sing, either. All it did was grow when he watered it, and shrivel when he didn't.

This was not nearly enough for such a goodhearted magician, who wanted to give his heart and soul to his friend, the flower.

Again, the magician wondered, "Is this the way to treat a good magician? How come this pretty little flower isn't responding? Perhaps I should make more flowers? Perhaps they will return my friendship"?

So the magician made all kinds of plants:
meadows with carpets of red, yellow, and
blue flowers, groves and forests,
vast savannas, and dense jungles.
But no matter what kind of plant
he made, they all behaved just
like the very first flower.

Once again, the good magician
was alone, and sad.

Realizing that the situation
called for special action,
the magician sat on his magic thinking rock.

He thought,
and thought,
and thought some more,
until he had a wonderful idea:

"I know," he said out loud,
"I'll make an animal!
But... what kind of animal?

Perhaps a dog?

Yes, a dog!
I'll make a cute little pup that
will always be with me.

I'll take it for walks,
play with it,
and when I return
to my castle,
the dog will jump for joy
and wiggle its tail
to greet me.

"Yes!" the magician
smiled to himself, the dog
and I will be very happy
together...

because it's
very sad
to be alone.

Hopeful, the magician waved his magic stick, and CHACK!

a cute little puppy
rested in his hands,
exactly as he
had pictured it.

The good magician was elated; he fed the dog,
cuddled and caressed its soft, curly fur. He took it
on walks and even gave it bubble baths. For sure,
this was the most spoiled pup ever.

But after some time, the magician realized
that a dog's love was not the kind of love he wanted.
A dog just wants to sit next to its owner and obey its owner.

The magician was very sad to see that even such a
cute little pup that played so cheerfully and followed
him wherever he went, still couldn't return all the
goodheartedness that he wanted to give it.

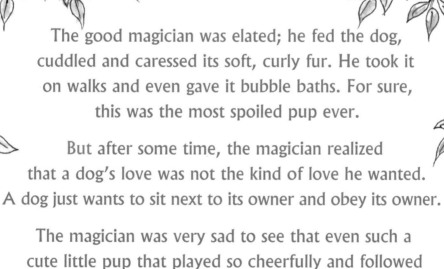

He realized that a dog
just couldn't be the kind of friend
that he was looking for.

It couldn't understand
the things he did for it,
how he cared for his dog,
and how he troubled
with the food and games
he had made for it.

The dog
could not appreciate all that,
and this was
what the magician
really needed,
a friend who would
appreciate his kindness
and good heart.

As with the pebble and the flower,
the magician made many other kinds of animals:
beetles, fish, snakes, monkeys, birds, and bears.
Still, not a single animal could understand
him and be the friend he was seeking.

Again, the magician was sad,
and very much alone.

And once again, the magician turned to his thinking rock
to determine what to do.
He thought, and thought,
and thought really hard.
This time, he had a whole plan worked out:
he realized that a true friend must be someone
who would search for him as much as he was searching,
someone who would want to find him as much as he
wanted to find his friend.

Then, after some more thinking,
he said to himself:
"A friend must be
someone like me,
who does what I do, and loves the way I love.
That's the only way he could really understand me.

But, to be like me he would have to
understand and appreciate
what I am giving him.
This way, he could return my love
and do for me what I will do for him.

Then, we would both be happy."

For three days and three nights
the magician sat on his magic rock
and thought about his next creation.

Finally, he had a brilliant idea!

"Why don't I make a man?
Yes, what a great idea!
He could be my true friend!
He could be just like me!

If I make him just right,
he will love what I love,
and appreciate what I will give him.
He'll just need a little bit of help
and then we will be
very happy
because we'll never be alone."

But to be happy, the
magician knew,
his friend would first need
to feel what it was like
being alone and
without a friend.
Actually, he would
have to feel what it was
like being without the
magician's
friendship.

With new hope in his heart,
the magician waved his magic stick
for the fourth, and last time, and CHACK!

But this time, two things
happened: a man was made, but
he was made in a very
far away land.
So far away was that land,
the man didn't even know
about the magician.
He saw the mountains, the stars,
the trees, the flowers, the fish,
and the animals, but he didn't
know that it was the magician who
made them. He didn't even know
there was a magician!

But the magician did not stop there.
He made a computer, football, basketball,
and all kinds of games so the man,
his new friend, would enjoy himself.
But all the while, the magician was
still alone and very sad
because his friend didn't know
about him.

The man didn't know that there was a magician who had made him, who loved him, and waited for him.

He didn't know that the magician was whispering, "Come, join me, we can be happy together, because it's truly very sad to be alone."

But how can someone who
doesn't know the magician, and
has a computer, football, and
all kinds of fun things to do,
suddenly want to find him?
How can someone like that even
want to know and love him?
Can such a person be the
magician's true friend,
and tell him,

"**Come**, my good magician, let's
be together and happy, because
I know how sad it is to be alone"?

The man knew only what he
saw around him.
He wanted to have what
others had, do what others
did, and talk about what
others talked about.
He didn't know that
somewhere out there was a
good magician, who was sad
to be alone.

Well, our magician is a clever one;
he had a plan in mind.
In fact, he'd had it all along and he
was only waiting for the right moment
to carry it out.

And one sunny day,
the right moment came:
the magician stood very far from
his friend, and very softly whispered
straight into his friend's
heart: **CHACK!**

He touched his heart with his magic
stick, **CHACK!** and once again...
A voice was calling in the
man's heart.

CHACK!

And when the magician "Chack'd"
   with his magic stick once more,
      the man began to think,
"Hah, there is a magician!
      Hmmm... very interesting,
      I wonder what he's like."

All of a sudden, **the man began to think**
   that perhaps it wasn't that much fun being
without a magician in his life, that he would
      actually be much happier with him.

CHACK!

Then the magician "Chack'd" again
and the man suddenly felt that somewhere, very far away, there was a land.
And in that land was a tower filled with treasures.
And in that tower sat a wise and kind magician, just waiting for him.
And the magician was whispering, "Hello, friend, I am waiting for you;
together, we will be happy, and alone we will be sad."

But the man didn't know where to find the land with the tower in it.
He didn't even know which way to look for it.
The man was sad and confused; he wondered,

"How do I meet the magician?"

And all the while that gentle tap was
patting in his heart:
CHACK!   CHACK!

He couldn't sleep,
he couldn't eat, and
he couldn't stop imagining
that tall tower in his mind.

That's what happens when
you search for something
really hard but can't find it.
It can make you very sad
to be alone.

But a "Chack!" was not enough for that. This was something the man had to do by himself.

For the man to be as wise as the magician, as powerful and goodhearted, the magician had to teach him how to do the same wonders he himself could do.

To help him, the magician gently and secretly led him to an ancient magical book, called *The Book of Zohar*. This book taught the man the way to the high tower in the faraway land.

Following the instructions in the book, the man rushed to meet his friend, the magician. He wanted to tell him, "Hello! I've come to be with you; I know we will be happy together."

But when the man reached the tower, he discovered that all around it was a high wall, surrounded by scary guards. They pushed him away every time he tried to approach and wouldn't let the man and the magician meet, much less be together.

And the more the man insisted, the tougher and more forceful the guards became. They had no mercy.

The man was in despair. His dear friend, the magician, was hidden in the tower, the gates were locked, the wall was high, and the mean guards kept pushing him away. No one could enter and no one could leave the tower.

The man thought, "What am I going to do? If we cannot be together, how will we ever be happy?"

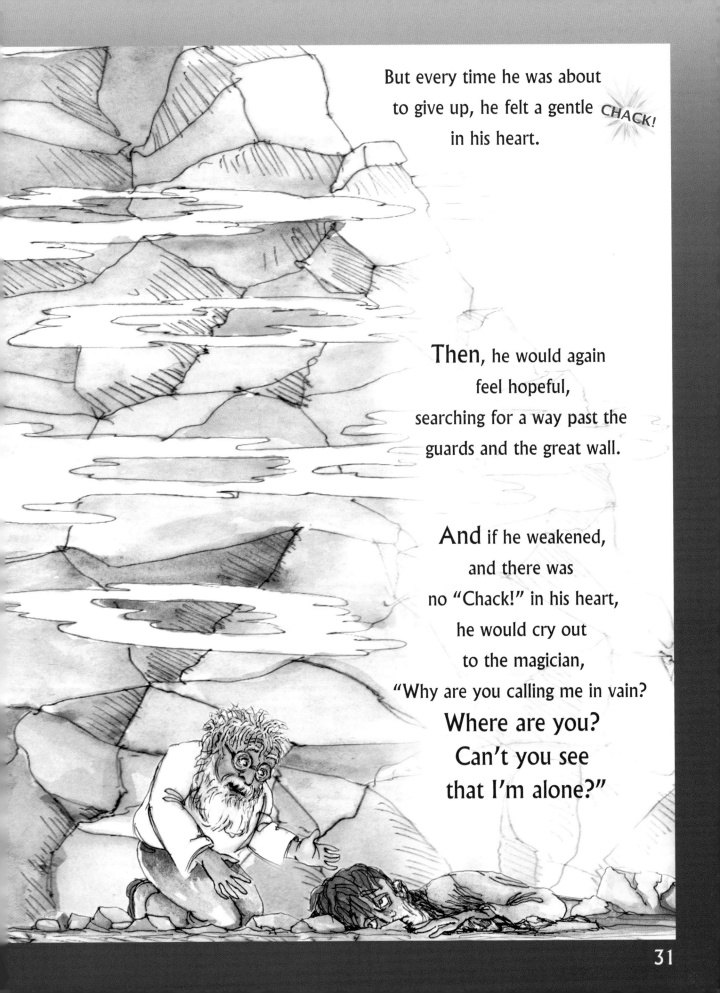

But every time he was about
to give up, he felt a gentle CHACK!
in his heart.

Then, he would again
feel hopeful,
searching for a way past the
guards and the great wall.

And if he weakened,
and there was
no "Chack!" in his heart,
he would cry out
to the magician,
"Why are you calling me in vain?
**Where are you?
Can't you see
that I'm alone?"**

Yet, if a person is patient and endures the beating
of the guards, he becomes stronger, braver,
and wiser. Instead of growing weaker, he learns to
do his own magic, his own wonders,
like only a magician can.
And this is what the man did, too.

Finally, after all that
had happened, there was
nothing the man wanted
more than to be with his
friend, the magician.
All he now wanted was
to see his friend, because
he was still alone.

And just when he felt he couldn't bear being alone for even one more minute, the gates of the tower suddenly opened. And yes, the great magician, his goodhearted, kind friend, came to meet him, and said, **"Come**, let's be together, because it's very sad to be alone."

And ever since that day, they have been the best of friends, **together forever.** There is no greater joy than the joy of their friendship.

And the wonder of their love is eternal;
it lives forever, and ever, and ever.
And they are so happy being together, that they don't even remember, not even sometimes, how sad it was to be alone.

So if you ever feel a gentle "Chack!" deep in your heart, know that there is a kind and wise magician calling you, because he wants to be your friend.

After all, it can be very sad to be alone.

THE END!

HOW TO CONTACT BNEI BARUCH

1057 Steeles Avenue West, Suite 532
Toronto, ON, M2R 3X1
Canada

194 Quentin Rd, 2nd floor
Brooklyn, New York, 11223
USA

E-mail: info@kabbalah.info
Web site: www.kabbalah.info

Toll free in USA and Canada:
1-866-LAITMAN
Fax: 1-905 886 9697